GOOD DOG, CARL

By
Alexandra Day

Aladdin Paperbacks

To H.D., who has never let us forget about Ponies

First Aladdin Paperbacks edition August 1997
Copyright © 1985 by Alexandra Day

Aladdin Paperbacks
An imprint of Simon & Schuster Children's Publishing Division
1230 Avenue of the Americas, New York, NY 10020

Also available in a Simon & Schuster Books for Young Readers edition.
22 24 26 28 30 29 27 25 23 21
Library of Congress Cataloging-in-Publication Data

Day, Alexandra
Good dog, Carl / by Alexandra Day.
— 1st Aladdin Paperbacks ed.
p.   cm.
Summary: Lively and unusual things happen when
Carl the dog is left in charge of the baby.
ISBN-13: 978-0-689-81771-7 (pbk.)   ISBN-10: 0-689-81771-1 (pbk.)
[1. Babies—Fiction. 2. Dogs—Fiction.
3. Babysitters—Fiction. 4. Stories without words.]
I. Title
PZ7.D32915Gp   1997 [E]—dc21
97-18516 CIP AC
Manufactured in China
1010 KWO

"Look after the baby, Carl.
I'll be back shortly."

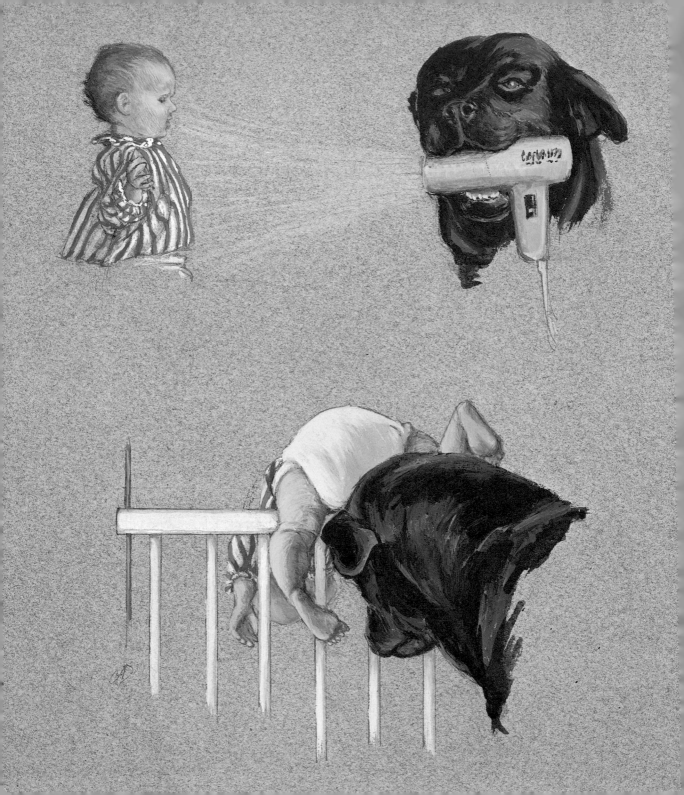

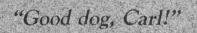

"Good dog, Carl!"

*A salute to the creator of Münchener Bilderbogen No. 1001,
and thanks to Molly Myers and Toby for their sitting talent.*

The paintings for this book were executed in egg tempera.
Color separations by Photolitho, AG, Gossau/Zurich, Switzerland.
Printed and bound in China.